W9-AAE-202

STRIPED ICE CREAM

JOAN M. LEXAU

Interior illustrations by John Wilson

A
LITTLE APPLE
PAPERBACK

SCHOLASTIC INC.
New York Toronto London Auckland Sydney

No part of this publication may be reproduced in whole or in part, or stored in a retrieval system, or transmitted in any form or by any means, electronic, mechanical, photocopying, recording, or otherwise, without written permission of the publisher. For information regarding permission, write to HarperCollins Children's Books, a division of HarperCollins Publishers, Inc., 10 East 53rd Street, New York, NY 10022.

ISBN 0-590-45729-2

21 20 19 18 17 16 15   1 2/0

Printed in the U.S.A.   40

To my friend
Rosa Velez

CONTENTS

A Surprise for Mama

"AND EVERY LAST ONE of you needs new shoes," Mama said. She was going through their clothes to find out what still fit them. School began in a few weeks.

The five of them stood before her looking guilty. Cecily was fourteen and the oldest and getting to be a young lady. She was in charge when Mama was at work, but Cecily wasn't as bossy as she might have been. Florence was thirteen, shy away from home, but she knew her own mind. Abe, the only boy, was eleven.

He spent as much time as he could playing outside. "Too many girls around here," he always said. Maude was ten but she tried to act as if she were as old as Flo and Cecily.

The youngest was Rebecca Jane, nearly eight, who always felt very much out of things and who spent a lot of time thinking that no matter how old she got, she would never catch up to the others.

Mama looked at their guilty faces and said, "I know you can't help it, growing out of things or wearing them out. But I don't know how I'm going to get new shoes for all of you."

"It's my fault," Abe said.

"Nobody said it was your fault," his mother said.

Becky was thinking, if school was coming soon, so was her birthday. Did they remember? "Mama — " she said.

"Well, if I hadn't gotten sick last winter, you wouldn't have had to spend all that money on medicine and stuff," Abe said.

"There are always things to spend money on," his mother said. "All I ask is that you have the sense to wear your coat and something on your head."

"Mama — " Becky said.

"In this heat?" Abe said.

"You know what I mean," his mother said. "In winter."

Cecily said, "I can't watch him all the time. He runs out before I know it."

"Mama — " Becky said.

Mama said, "He's old enough to know better."

"OK, OK," Abe said.

"Mama — " Becky said and waited. No one said anything. They all looked at her. "My birthday's coming pretty soon," she said. "Will we have chicken-spaghetti and striped ice cream? It's what we had on my birthday last year." Mama had cooked a little chicken and cut it up in small pieces in the spaghetti.

Her mother sighed. Becky wished she

hadn't said anything. This was not the time to bring up birthdays.

"I don't know, Becky," Mama said. "Things were a little better last year. And with Cecily getting older, she should have more school dresses. I've been thinking about that. I could get some material that doesn't cost too much at the remnant store. If we could all learn to sew —"

"I'm sure we could," Cecily said.

"I'll help," Flo said. "I'd like to learn how to sew."

"Me too," Maude said.

"Me too, me too," Becky yelled. "I bet I could sew."

"Do I have to learn?" Abe asked.

"Of course not," Mama said. "And, Becky, I don't want you staying inside sewing. It's bad enough the older girls have to work so hard. I want you to play while you can. I found some work for tomorrow that will help a little. One of the women at work said that her cousin was giving a party Sunday. She's always talking about her rich cousin. So I asked if her cousin could use some help at the party. She called her up at lunch time and asked her. Her cousin didn't need any help on Sunday but she could use some help tomorrow cleaning. So that's what I'll be doing. I don't have to be there till late in the morning so, Cecily, if you want to come with me as far as the remnant store, we can look at material."

No one said anything more about Becky's birthday. Becky went to bed in a very bad mood. She didn't mind not getting presents, she was used to that, but they always had something nice to eat on their birthdays. Now they'd probably forget her birthday. Shoes and dresses, that's all that mattered. She'd like to have a new dress once in a while. By the time the dresses came down to her, they looked worn and faded. The only good thing about them was they always had matching buttons. Mama worked in a button factory and could bring home seconds. Becky was tired of faded, patched-up dresses.

At breakfast the next morning all the children helped their mother clean the apartment as they always did on Saturday. It was Becky's week for making the bed where she slept with Maude and Flo. It was the job she hated most. Only one person could do it at a time because the room was so small that there was only a little space between the bed and the wall. Part of the time she had to be on the bed itself to make it so it was hard to do a good job. If she left any wrinkles, Maude made a big fuss. At least, Becky thought, it was the end of her week. Next week, starting tomorrow, it would be Flo's turn again.

She scrubbed the bedroom floor, another job she hated. She had to crawl under the bed to scrub under it. Sometimes she forgot where she'd left off and crawled around in the wet. The first time she had scrubbed this floor, she had started at the door and scrubbed herself into a corner under the bed. She'd had to wait there until the floor dried. All the others had stood in the doorway laughing until Mama made them stop. She never did that again.

Cecily and Mama were washing clothes in the bathtub to save the money they would have spent at the Laundromat. They had to save every penny they could until all the shoes were bought.

While Flo got to work on the kitchen floor, Becky and Abe dusted in the living room. Abe moved his cloth so fast that he left half the dust. Becky dusted again after him and he grinned and said, "OK, I'll do it right, Becky." Then they got out of the way while Flo and Maude washed the living-room floor. A good part of Saturday mornings was spent in getting out of the way of someone doing floors.

With so many of them to do the work, it didn't take long. Pretty soon the clothes were hung on the line in the courtyard and Mama was ready to go off to her job.

She said, "Cecily, do you want to come with me now to the remnant store to see if there is some material you like?"

"I'm going to work with you, Mama. I can help," Cecily said.

"I am, too," Abe said. "I can lift things."

Then they all wanted to go. Mama said, "All right, Abe, you and Cecily can come with me, but the rest of you stay home and be good."

Becky was glad that Flo had to stay home too. When she and Maude were alone, there was always a fight because Maude was bossy.

Mama gave them the phone number at Mrs. Robbin's house. Their phone cost a lot of money but when Mama was at work, she didn't want to be out of reach of her children if they got sick or hurt. The phone was almost never used but it was there.

As soon as Mama left, Flo said, "Let's surprise Mama. Let's wash all the curtains and iron them before they get back."

They carried the kitchen table from window

to window. Flo climbed on it and took the curtains down. In their bedroom she had to climb on the bed. When the first pair of curtains was in the tub and Flo and Maude were scrubbing them, Flo frowned and said, "I don't know if they'll dry in time in here. The outside line is all full."

Becky said quickly, "Let's take the clothes down from outside and put them on the rack over the tub. Then we can hang the curtains outside."

"I was just about to say that," Maude said.

"You were not," Becky said.

"Never mind," Flo said. "It's a good idea."

"I'll take them down now," Becky said.

"You'll drop them," Maude said. "Then we'd have to go downstairs and get them and wash them over. I'll take them in."

So Becky stooped over the tub and started washing curtains. Maude let the rack down and hung the clothes on it. Water dripped down on them as they worked.

It seemed to take forever but at last the curtains were hung outside. They had dripped so much water on the floor in the bathroom and on the way to the kitchen window to hang out the curtains that they had to mop again. By that time they were glad to sit down and rest.

Becky looked at the windows and thought how surprised their mother would be when she found out they'd washed the curtains.

"You know what," she said, "we could wash the windows too."

"I'm tired," Maude said.

"You don't have to help," Becky said. "Flo and I can do it."

"I didn't say I wouldn't help," Maude said. "I just said I was tired. Let's get started."

"Just the insides," Flo told them. "Mama would never forgive me if one of you fell out the window. I'll do the top parts and you two can do the lower parts."

Once more the kitchen table made the rounds as they washed and rinsed and dried

the windows. They had to mop up again when they were done with each window.

"I wish we'd left the floors till last," Becky said.

"They ought to be good and clean now," Maude said.

By the time they had rested again, some of the curtains were nearly dry. They began ironing, taking turns. They let Becky help, too, because the curtains were flat easy pieces. Flo watched her closely.

They had had only sandwiches for lunch and they were hungry. They didn't know what time Mama would come home, but they waited supper for her.

The Goodwill Bag

MAMA AND CECILY AND ABE didn't get home until ten. Abe and Mama were carrying a huge bag between them.

"Man, am I beat!" Abe said. He flopped down on the couch.

"So are all of us," Cecily said.

"Why don't you rest then? Maude and Becky and I will cook supper," Flo said.

"Didn't you girls eat?" Mama asked.

"No. We waited for you," Flo said.

"You know what, Mama — " Becky began.

"Hush," Flo said.

"I ate but I'm hungry again," said Abe.

Mama said, "I think we could all stand to eat something. Why don't you girls start supper, Flo?"

Becky opened her mouth again but Flo took her by the arm and led her to the kitchen. Maude followed.

"Why don't you want me to tell her what we did?" Becky asked, as she began to set the table.

"Because," Flo said, "if I know Mama, she'd say we must be tired and she would make supper. She must be more tired than we are. Let's tell her tomorrow."

Flo put the spaghetti in the big pot and Maude opened a can of spaghetti sauce. Abe came out and sat at the table. "Spaghetti, huh?" he said. "We had chicken chow mein. Mrs. Robbin sent out for it. Chow mein and rice and some funny soup."

"Abe, you didn't have to tell them that," Cecily said, coming in. She opened a paper bag and took something out of it. "But look what Mrs. Robbin gave us to take home. We were too full to eat it. You know, she gave Mama ten dollars and she gave Abe and me two dollars each and this too." She put a package of frozen brownies on the table.

"Do they look good!" Maude said.

"Can I see your money?" Becky asked Cecily.

"I gave it to Mama," Cecily said. "Abe did, too. It's shoe money."

"What's in that big bag?" Becky said, hoping it was something nice.

"It's a Goodwill bag," Cecily said. "I don't know what's in it. Mrs. Robbin said there might be something in it we could use. She made it sound like such a favor to her for getting it off her hands and not like charity or anything so we took it. I don't know what's in it but we'll find out right after supper."

"There should be something good in it," Abe said. "You should see their house. Wow! They're so rich they've got furniture in sets. Like, in the living room all the furniture goes together. They must have bought it new all at one time. And she's got three kids and they're away at camp for the whole summer."

"And the dishes," Cecily said. "They've got dishes they just use for good. We had to take them down from a high cupboard and wash them. And Mrs. Robbin kept thanking us and asked if we could come back again sometime when she was going to have a party."

"Yeah, but we did work hard," Abe said.

"So did — " Becky began. Flo gave her a look.

Supper went quickly because they were in a hurry to see what was in the bag. Mama let them eat half the brownies and saved the rest for the next day.

While they were eating, Flo asked Cecily, "Did you see some nice material at the store?"

"Yes, I did," Cecily said. "The man put it aside for us. I'm going to buy it Monday with some of the money we made today."

As soon as they finished eating, they began a rush for the living room to open the bag. Mama said the dishes had to be done first.

Becky said, "Can't we leave them till tomorrow?"

Mama said, "Do you want the bugs to have a party? Do the dishes first and we'll wait."

"She's just trying to get out of them," Maude said. "It isn't her turn any more tomorrow."

It was Flo and Becky's week to do the dishes but Maude helped Becky dry because she was in such a hurry. "You're so slow, Becky," she said.

Why can't she just help without saying something nasty, Becky thought, but she didn't say it. It would only start a fight.

When the dishes were done, Mama began to take things out of the bag. Right on top was a little paper bag. It was full of buttons, matched and unmatched. This started them all giggling.

"Just what we needed," Mama said.

Next came a broken alarm clock. "Maybe I can fix it," Abe said.

"No. Better not mess with it," Mama said. "Maybe some day we can take it to have it fixed."

"I hope everything isn't broken," Flo said.

Mama pulled out an iron. They all gathered around it.

"It's a steam iron," Cecily said.

"How much you want to bet it doesn't work?" Abe said.

"Let's try it," Flo yelled.

"Hush. Remember the neighbors. It's late," Mama said. "All right, now, all of you stand back while I plug it in. There might be something wrong with the wiring."

But Abe took it away from her before she knew what he was doing.

"You let a man take care of this," he said. He plugged it in. They waited to see what would happen.

At first nothing did. "Broken. I knew it," Abe said.

"No, it's getting warm, it's getting warm," Flo said.

"It does work," Cecily said. "It looks pretty new. I wonder why she threw it out."

Mama said, "It may have been a mistake. I'll call her tomorrow and ask."

"It's not our fault if she made a mistake," Maude said.

"If she didn't mean to give it away, it's still hers," Mama said. "I'll ask her."

Next came a baseball glove. There was no doubt about who should have that.

Mama took out a figurine of a red bird with just a little chip off one wing. Cecily took it in her hands and looked at it longingly.

"That isn't fair," Maude said. "What if there isn't anything else in there for me?"

Becky had been thinking the same thing. She was glad she hadn't said it.

Mama said, "We'll see how it works out when we're all through." She pulled out a pair of boy's shoes, still whole. They each tried them on. The shoes fit Maude.

"I'm not going to wear these to school," Maude said.

"You don't have to," Mama said. "You can wear them for play."

Next was a green velvet dress with a hat to match.

"Ohh!" Becky gasped but she knew it was too big for her. Maude held it against herself but it was too large. It fit Flo. Maude pouted.

Flo said, "You'll have it next, Maudie. I'll take good care of it. And you have that nice blue party dress Mama found at the rummage sale."

Becky was near to tears.

Cecily said, "Never mind, Becky. You'll have a nice dress some day."

Becky tried to smile. It was nice of Cecily to say so, but it was silly, too, because it wouldn't ever happen.

The velvet dress had been wrapped around a small framed picture of a mountain with snow on top. "Isn't that pretty," Flo said. "Let's hang it in the living room."

Mama pulled three aprons out of the bag. They were too large for her but she said she

would wear them to work anyway. There was another little paper bag. Inside it was a pair of pearl earrings and a pin shaped like a horse.

"Mama should have the earrings," Cecily said.

"Where would I wear them?" Mama said. "No, it's time you had a little jewelry to wear for special."

"Becky hasn't had anything yet," Flo said. "She should have the pin."

"She can have the shoes," Maude said, but they didn't answer her.

Maude felt better when she found that a pair of red play-shorts fit her. Next came a long green corduroy robe that was too small for Flo and a little too big for Maude. When Maude tried it on, she found a small hole in it and frowned, but she hung on to it.

A pair of striped pajamas fit Abe and also a pair of blue jeans worn at the knee. "Hah, they match my other pair, holes and all," Abe said.

"I'll patch them up," Mama said.

When Mama pulled out a boy's shirt with a small burn from an iron in the collar, Cecily said, "I'll turn the collar for you, Abe."

"I don't care about a little burn," Abe said.

"Well, I do," said Cecily. "I don't want people thinking I did it."

There was a pair of sneakers that were too large for Abe but Mama said they could put newspaper in them. There was also a pair of brown trousers Abe's size, good enough for school. "That's one thing we don't have to buy," Mama said.

A yellow cotton dress fit Flo.

"I knew it," Maude said.

"You have enough dresses," Mama said. "Some of them are still good when they get to you. It's Becky who gets the worst of it."

Next came a yellow umbrella, still in its

case. "I'd better ask Mrs. Robbin about this as well," Mama said. "You don't outgrow an umbrella."

"If it wasn't a mistake, can I have it?" Maude asked.

"Mama should have it," Flo said.

"We can all share it," Mama said.

There were two terry dish towels with roosters on them. Inside the dish towels was a pair of bookends with dog heads on them.

"We can put our library books in them," Abe said.

Next Mama pulled out a plastic raincoat with red and yellow flowers on it and a scarf to match.

"If that fits Flo, I'll scream," Maude said.

"Here, you try it on first," Flo said.

It was a little big on her but all agreed that Maude should have it.

Maude said, "We're nearly at the bottom of the bag and it looks like there isn't anything real nice for you except the pin, Becky. Here, you can have this." She handed the robe to Becky.

Becky put it on. It was much too big, but she didn't care. She didn't care if there was a hole in it.

"Look, Becky's a princess," Flo said.

For a minute Becky thought Maude was going to ask for the robe back, but Mama said, "That was very nice of you, Maude," and Maude smiled.

Mama pulled a black purse from the bag and said, "Now I can stop sewing up the handle on my old one."

When they all saw the book of fairy tales, the fight began. Even Cecily joined in.

Mama told them if they didn't shush at once, she'd send them all to bed. When they were quiet, she said, "Do you want to take turns with this book or should we throw it out?" They all agreed to take turns. Cecily, as the oldest, would have it first.

Next was a first-grade reader which all the others turned up their noses at. Becky was glad to have it. At the bottom of the bag were two big boxes of picture puzzles. A fight might have started over these but they knew what would happen.

"Turns," Abe said. "I get first turn."

"We can work them together," Flo said. "We don't need turns on these."

"I hope the pieces are all there," Cecily said.

Maude said, trying on the raincoat once more, "Well, I don't care if it is charity. I like it."

Mama said, "There's charity and there's charity. The word means love, you know. Mrs. Robbin knows how to give things so she doesn't hurt your feelings. And remember that woman who came when Abe was in the hospital to check that we really couldn't pay? She knew she put my back up when she said we should go on Welfare. She didn't say any more about it. But she saw how things were with us then, with the medicine and the time I had to take off work and everything. The next day that five dollars came in an envelope with no name and return address so we couldn't send it back. Out of her own pocket, that was. Now that was real charity."

"She was nice," Cecily said.

"Yes, but even she called me by my first name," Mama said. "Didn't even know me but she thought it was all right to call me by my first name. Most likely she didn't even think about it."

"How come we don't go on Welfare?" Abe asked. "Then you could stay home. You wouldn't have to go to work. And we wouldn't have things so hard."

"Things would be even harder," Mama said. "You don't get that much from Welfare. And they think they own you then. They own your souls. We can make out ourselves somehow and still feel human. Now, to bed with you right away. I shouldn't have let you stay up this late but I guess just this once it doesn't hurt."

"It was just like Christmas," Becky said. "Wasn't it? Or a birthday party." Now she wouldn't feel so bad if they didn't have anything special to eat on her birthday. It just couldn't be helped, that was all.

People Hurt People Sometimes

BECKY WAS SO EXCITED she didn't know if she could sleep. She slept next to the wall, with Flo in the middle. Becky had slept in the middle at one time but Maude used to kick her and then say when Becky yelled that she did it in her sleep. So at last Flo said she would sleep in the middle or they'd be up every night. Maude kicked Flo just once and found herself on the floor. She never did it again. Tonight they were still awake and talking about the new things when Mama came in.

"All right, who did it?" Mama demanded.

Becky tried to think back to what she could have done wrong.

"What is it, Mama?" Flo asked.

Mama gave up trying to look mad. She laughed and said, "Who did the curtains? I was just going to turn out the light when I thought something looked funny about the windows. I saw what had happened. Then I looked at the window in the kitchen."

"We all did it," Flo said.

"And the insides of the windows, too," Becky said.

"You did all that work and never said a word about it!" Mama said. "Well, you have a very grateful mother. Now go to sleep. No more talking."

The next morning after breakfast, they got ready for church. Abe put on his shoes and said, "Look, holey shoes for a holy day."

Mama said, "Put on your new sneakers, Abe. They look better than those shoes."

That afternoon it rained. "Mama, can I wear my raincoat, can I?" asked Maude. "I'll keep it nice."

"All right," Mama said, laughing. "Walk around in it and show it off if you have to."

Becky tried not to stare at the raincoat. Some day, she told herself, some day I'll have it. But that would be a long time because the coat was big on Maude now. It would be a long time before she outgrew it. It was hard to think ahead to "some day" anyway.

Just as Maude was about to start out, Mama said, "Wait a minute." She went to the phone and called Mrs. Robbin. When she hung up the phone, she told them, "She really meant to throw out the iron and the umbrella. She said they always have too many umbrellas and she got a newer iron as a gift."

Taking the case off, she handed the umbrella to Becky. "Here, Becky, why don't you walk around the block with Maude," she said.

"Thank you, Mama," Becky said. Mama always seemed to know when she was feeling sad and tried to do something about it.

"Isn't this fun?" Maude said as they walked down the street. "I wish somebody we knew was outside so they could see us. But all the kids are inside."

"Yes," Becky said. "They're in because it's raining and we're out because it's raining."

When they were nearly home, Maude ducked into the doorway of a store. "Come here, Becky," she said. She took off the raincoat and scarf. "Now you can have a turn," she said. "I'll take the umbrella."

Maude could be nice sometimes, Becky thought. The coat was nearly down to her ankles and it was hot but she didn't care. It was funny to walk in the rain and not worry about your clothes getting wet. She looked up and let the cool rain fall on her face.

"Look out!" Maude said. "You nearly walked in a puddle. Better look where you're going."

"I bet mud would wipe right off this coat," Becky said. There was water squishing around in her shoes. She wished she had asked Mama if she could have gone out barefoot.

When they got home, dinner was ready.

"Oh, boy, beans and wieners," Becky said. The wieners were cut up in the beans. It was one of her favorite meals. "I wouldn't mind having this — " she began and stopped. No, she wasn't going to say any more about her birthday. If Mama couldn't have anything special on her birthday, it would make her feel bad if Becky kept talking about it.

"Enjoy it," Mama said. "We won't have anything this good for a while. We have to save up for school."

After they ate up all the beans and wieners and the brownies, and the dishes were done, Mama ironed. All the others but Cecily sat on the floor to do one of the picture puzzles. Cecily sat on the couch with the fairy-tale book.

"Would you like me to read it out loud?" she asked them.

"No," said Maude. "I want to read it by myself."

Flo and Abe and Becky said they wanted to hear it.

Maude went off to her room. "Don't read too loud. I don't want to hear it," she said.

Cecily began to read *Little Red Riding Hood* and they forgot about the picture puzzle. They sat there taking in every word. Becky looked away when Cecily was turning a page and saw Maude in the doorway. The next time Becky looked around, Maude was sitting with them.

After a while, Cecily ironed and Mama sat down and read from the book. Mama read more slowly than Cecily and now and then she stopped to ask questions.

She was reading *The Princess on the Glass Hill*. She asked, "If the hill was so steep and slippery, how did the princess get on the top?"

"Maybe she had a helicopter," Becky said.

"They didn't have helicopters then," Abe told her.

"Maybe she went up a ladder," Maude said.

"That big a ladder?" Mama asked. "To go up a hill?"

"Well, a princess could have a ladder that long, couldn't she?" Maude said.

Cecily said, "It could have been magic, Mama. A lot of things happen by magic in the stories."

"Yes, you can have anything happen by magic in a story," Mama said. "That's too easy. I like a story that makes sense. Was it magic in *Little Red Riding Hood*? I didn't want to stop you to say something, Cecily. But if the wolf had the grandmother's nightcap over his face, how could Red Riding Hood see his eyes to say, 'What big eyes you have'?"

"Oh, Mama, please just *read!*" Flo said. "I want to know what happens."

Mama went back to her reading. Becky missed part of the story because she was thinking about what Mama had said about Red Riding Hood. At last she sighed. She couldn't figure it out. She wished Mama hadn't said it.

The afternoon went by quickly. In the evening they had vegetable soup and milk. Mama went back to the ironing while Becky and Abe worked on the puzzle. Cecily and Flo were doing the dishes and Maude was in the kitchen talking to them.

Becky picked up a piece of the puzzle and tried to fit it in. Abe took it from her.

"See, Becky, that goes over here," he said.

"Let me find out myself," Becky said. "You've got all those other pieces. You can find places for them. You don't have to take mine."

"It would take a million years to do the puzzle at the rate you're going," Abe said.

"No fighting," Mama said.

Becky got up and walked away.

"C'mon back, Becky," Abe said. "I didn't mean it. I just wanted to help you."

Becky didn't answer. She went to the kitchen to see what the girls were talking about. She heard Cecily say, "I'm sure we can do it in time if we all help like crazy."

"What about Abe?" Maude said. "He should do something."

Cecily said, "He can keep Becky out of our hair."

This wasn't like Cecily at all. Becky could hardly believe it. But Cecily had said it. Becky went in and shouted, "Cecily-Silly, I'll stay out of your hair all right." She was so angry, she didn't know what more to say. She tried to think of something really bad.

Flo said, "Becky, you shouldn't listen when other people are talking."

"I'll listen all I please!" Becky screamed.

"Anyway, who wants to listen to your dumb talk."

Mama came rushing out. "What's going on?" she said. "What is it?"

Maude said, "She was listening to us and we were talking about — "

"We were talking about getting my dress done in time for school," Cecily said.

"Becky lives here too," Mama said.

"She doesn't have to sneak up on people," said Maude.

Becky burst into tears and went to her room. Cecily came running after her.

"Don't cry, Baby," she said. "I'm sorry. I shouldn't have said what I did."

Becky buried her head in her pillow and howled.

All of them were trying to crowd into the room.

Abe said, "Come and help me with the puzzle, Becky. I don't want to do it all by myself."

"Do you want to look at the fairy-tale book?" Cecily asked.

Maude said, "The next time it rains, you can wear my raincoat around the block if you want."

"You can play my harmonica, Becky. I could teach you a song on it. Would you like that?" Flo asked.

Soon it was quiet and Becky knew they were gone, all but Mama. She knew that Mama would be there, looking sad.

Mama sat down on the bed beside her and waited until she had stopped crying. Mama said, "People hurt people sometimes and then they're sorry. You know it's bound to happen now and then."

"I know, Mama," Becky said. "But they do it so much. Just because they're all older, they treat me like a baby. I can't help it if I'm the youngest."

"Of course you can't, Becky," Mama said. "But you know they all love you. They all love you in a special way because you are the youngest."

Becky didn't know any such thing but she didn't want to tell Mama so. It would be like saying Mama was telling a lie. Mama must be just trying to make her feel better.

Becky sat up and dried her eyes with one hand.

"It's nearly bedtime," Mama said. "Why don't you get ready for bed and put your robe on? You know, you're the only one of us who has a robe. As soon as I can, I'll put a nail on the door so you can hang it there."

When Becky came out to the living room in her robe, Cecily said, "There's our Becky."

"Here comes the princess," Mama said.

"What would you like to do?" Flo asked Becky.

"I'd like Cecily to read some more," Becky said without looking at the others.

They sat down on the floor to hear Cecily read until bedtime.

When she was in bed, Becky couldn't help feeling sorry for herself. The others were always doing things she couldn't do. Last summer she had really felt bad when Cecily and Flo and Abe and Maude had gone swimming a couple of times and she had to stay home. Mama had tried to say it nice. She said that Becky wasn't used to the water and that she couldn't be sure the others would remember to keep an eye on her all the time. Then Maude had said, "How could we have any fun if we had to watch her every minute?"

There were so many times she was left out. Even Mama did it. Sometimes Mama would be talking to Cecily and stop talking when Becky came by. Once Becky said something about it and Mama said, "I'm not trying to keep secrets from you, Becky. It's just that there are things you're too little to have to worry about. Cecily helps me do my worrying."

The trouble was, Becky thought, she would always be the youngest. There was no way she could catch up. The others didn't stop to think how she felt. Maybe they just didn't know. How could they?

The No Parking Park

Becky held her doll close. She remembered when Maude had given up the doll at Christmas saying, "Here, Becky, I guess you should have it now." Sometimes Maude still looked at it longingly. Not long ago Becky had missed the doll one morning and found it in Maude's arms. The biggest fight she and Maude had ever had was when Becky wanted to change the doll's name from Marjorie to Lucinda. Maude had cried and screamed and carried on so much that Mama asked Becky to call the doll Marjorie Lucinda.

It wasn't much of a doll any more, being a hand-me-down like her clothes, but right now it was the only friend she had.

It was a hot night and Becky had a hard time falling asleep. She listened to the courtyard sounds. A man and his wife were yelling at each other, there was a TV going full blast, someone was doing dishes with a great clatter, and somewhere a window fan was humming loudly. Once a plane went low overhead and seemed to shake the building.

She lay as still as she could so she wouldn't keep Flo awake. But Flo whispered in her ear, "Can't you sleep, Baby?"

"No," Becky said crossly. They kept saying they wouldn't call her Baby any more and they kept forgetting.

"Shh, Maude's asleep," Flo whispered. "Shut your eyes and listen. Once upon a time there was a princess in a green robe who lived on top of a glass hill with her grandmother. One day a mean and hungry wolf made a long ladder and came up the hill — "

Becky fell asleep smiling.

When she woke up, Mama had already left for work and the others were eating breakfast.

Cecily put some cereal in a bowl for her.

"Hurry up and eat it while it's still hot," Flo said.

By the time Becky was through, the others had washed up their own dishes.

"We're going now, Becky," Flo said. "We're going to the store to buy the material and a pattern for Cecily's dress."

"You can go out and play with Abe," Maude said. "He'll wait for you, won't you, Abe?"

They were trying to get her out of the way and Becky knew it. Any other time she would have been glad to go with Abe.

"No, I think I'll go to the store," she said.

"Please, Becky," Cecily said, "please go with Abe. Will you do it for me?"

"Why should I?" Becky said.

"Because I'm asking," Cecily said.

Before she had time to think any more, Abe grabbed up his baseball glove and took her by the hand and led her out. They stopped for his friend Frank on the floor below and they went out to the park where they played three-sided catch.

Becky had trouble catching the ball. Even when she caught it, she dropped it because it stung her hands. One time it hit her finger and it hurt like mad. Abe and Frank were patient in trying to teach her and Abe threw the ball to her very gently.

She wasn't very good at throwing the ball to Frank. It was too high or it fell short. They tried to teach her to throw overhand but that was even worse. After a while Becky said,

"I don't want to do this any more. I want to go home."

Abe said, "Why don't you try out the glove? Let's see how that works. I'll throw the ball to you, Becky, and you throw it back to me and then I'll throw it to Frank."

Becky put the glove on. It was so big on her hand that she couldn't bend it. Abe threw the ball to her and she heard it land with a thwack in the glove. Then she looked around on the grass to see where it had fallen. Instead of helping her, Frank and Abe were doubled up laughing.

"Look," Abe gasped, "look in the glove, Becky." Becky looked and there was the ball, caught in the glove. She couldn't even feel it there.

Next they played fly ball. One of the boys threw the ball high in the air and they all tried to catch it. Becky didn't try very hard. She put the glove over her head so she wouldn't get bonked by the ball.

"Why don't you let me throw it?" she said. "Then I'll get out of the way and you can catch it."

They let her try it. It went all right at first but on the third throw, the ball landed in a tree. Abe had to climb up to get it.

All of a sudden, Frank said, "Hey, cheese it, the cops!"

"Are you kidding?" Abe said. "What do you want me to do, fly?"

Becky and Frank stayed because Abe couldn't leave. The policeman came over to them.

"What are you doing in that tree? You could fall and get hurt. Come down from there," the policeman said. Abe climbed down as fast as he could.

Becky was shaking but she said, "He can't help it. I threw the ball up there and he climbed up to get it."

The policeman came closer to her and she backed away. "What are you afraid of, young

lady?" he said. "I've got a little girl just your size. I wouldn't hurt you."

"I don't want you to put Abe in jail," Becky said.

"No one is going to jail," the policeman said. "But I do want to talk to all of you. Didn't you see that sign over there? It says No Ball Playing. You can see it isn't much of a place for playing ball anyway."

"Sure, and the sign also says no bicycles and no skates and no just about everything," Abe said. "You know what the sign on this park should say? It should say No Parking, that's what."

Becky was afraid the policeman might get mad but he didn't. He said, "See all those benches full of people? This park is a quiet place to sit. The people around here need a quiet place to get away from all the racket and rushing about. And they don't want to get hit on the head with a baseball."

Becky thought, it isn't such a quiet place when the trains go by. The railroad tracks were overhead at one side of the park. And there were trucks roaring down the street all the time.

The policeman went on, "Don't you know there's a playground two blocks over where you can play ball?"

"If you can get in it, you can," Abe said. "It's always full of older kids. About the only time I can play there is when it rains and even then sometimes there's a baseball game going on."

The policeman sighed. "I know," he said. "You're right. If I had my way, there'd be a place to play on every block. I guess the city hasn't got the room or the money. But rules are rules and they're all for a good reason. OK?"

"OK," Frank said.

"I guess so," Abe said.

"You still afraid of me?" the policeman asked Becky.

She shook her head. She wasn't as much afraid of him anyway, and she didn't want to hurt his feelings.

Becky was glad it was time to go home for lunch. When they got to their apartment, Abe knocked on the door.

"Don't you have your key?" Becky asked. "I've got mine."

"Never mind," Abe said. "Someone's coming."

There was a lot of giggling inside and then Maude opened the door.

"OK?" she called back over her shoulder.

"OK, let them in," Flo said.

Becky and Abe went in. Becky looked around to see what they had been doing. She couldn't see anything.

"I'll make you a sandwich, Becky," Cecily said. "What would you like, peanut butter or jelly?"

"And then," Maude cut in, "you can go out and stay out all afternoon."

"I'll make my own sandwich," Becky said. She put lots of peanut butter on and lots of jelly on top of it and waited for Cecily to tell her not to use so much, but Cecily didn't say a word. Becky ate as slowly as she could.

"Hurry up, Becky," Abe kept saying.

"Go on out," Becky told him. "You don't have to wait for me. I'm not playing with you this afternoon."

"But you have to," Maude said.

"No, she doesn't," Cecily said. "Becky, how would you like to take the fairy-tale book outside and read it in the park?"

Becky didn't answer.

Flo said, "Look, Becky, you know Mama said she didn't want you staying inside sewing."

"I could just watch for a while," Becky said.

"That would make us nervous," Cecily said.

"Sewing is hard work and we have to do a lot of thinking about it. So you go out and play. You're lucky you don't have to stay in and work."

Becky said, "Don't worry. I'll get out of your hair. And you can leave me alone, too." She wiped off the table and was ready to go out.

Just Dreaming

"WAIT, BECKY, I want to show you something," Cecily said. She went into the bedroom she and Mama shared and came back with a piece of red material. There was some tissue paper pinned to it. She spread it out on the table.

"See, this paper is the pattern, Becky," she said. "You have to pin it to the material just right and then cut around it. The lady at the dime store told us all about it. She even took the pieces of the pattern out to show us and she went over the instructions with us. We're going to wait until Mama comes home to cut it out. Mama says her grandmother helped her make a dress when she was my age and she hopes that she remembers something about it."

"I wish we had a sewing machine," Flo said. "Would the dress go fast then, I bet."

Becky still didn't know how she could bother them that much. Did she talk a lot when they were busy? She did like to talk, but they could always tell her to be quiet, couldn't they? After this, she thought, she would try not to talk so much. Then they would see she was not a bother to have around.

She said to Cecily, "I hope it comes out nice." Cecily handed her the fairy-tale book.

"What about when she comes back in?" Abe said.

"I'll *knock*," Becky said angrily. "Here, you can have my key." She took the string from around her neck and threw the key on the floor.

Cecily picked it up and handed it to her. "Just make some noise when you come in, Becky," she said.

Becky ran out. How could her coming in bother them? Maybe they had to think so hard working on the dress that her coming in would make them forget what they were doing. Still, making noise would bother them, too, then. But she couldn't stay out forever. It was her home, too.

She went to the park and looked around for the policeman. He was gone so she sat on a bench to read. There couldn't be a rule about that. It was so hot that after a while she had a better idea. She went to the library where there was a large fan. She asked the lady at the desk in the children's room if she could read her book there.

The lady said, "It's such a hot day out, I don't see why not."

Becky sat at one of the tables near the fan and opened the book. It was very hard going.

She couldn't make out some of the words. Soon she was tired of trying to read it. After she had looked at all the pictures, she closed the book and just sat there. She didn't want to go home and this was the coolest place she could think of.

The lady came over to her with a book. "Did you ever read this?" she asked. "It's one I like very much and I thought maybe you would too."

Becky took the book and thanked her. It was called *The Secret River.*

"The girl's name is Calpurnia," the lady said. "Her dog is called Buggy-horse." She went away.

Becky loved the story. It was about a girl who found a secret river and caught some fish in it. Her father needed the fish because there were hard times in the forest. When the hard times were over, Calpurnia couldn't find the river any more. But Becky wished the

river was real and not magic. What if the hard times came back?

The library was closing so it was time for Mama to come home. Becky waited for her at the corner. She liked to meet Mama and this way the others couldn't say she was bothering them coming in.

Supper was mashed potatoes and green beans.

"I don't like green beans," Abe said.

Mama said, "I know, but they were on special, and we're going to start buying shoes this Saturday. You'll need money after school starts, too, you know. You'll all be coming home needing fifty cents for this and fifty cents for that. It adds up even if your teachers don't seem to know it."

"Just so we don't have weeks of green beans," Abe said.

"How about beets?" Cecily asked him.

"Ugh!" said Abe. "I'd rather go hungry."

Mama said, "Wouldn't it be nice if you all liked the same things?"

"That's not the trouble," Flo said. "The trouble is we all hate different things. Abe can't stand beets and I can't stand spinach."

"What I like is tomatoes," Becky said. "I could eat them every night."

"So could we all, I think," Mama said, "but they cost so much."

Cecily said, "What we need is a house in the country with a garden."

"What we need is a million dollars," Abe said.

"Everything will be fine when our ship comes in," Mama said, smiling.

At one time Becky had thought Mama meant a real ship, that some day a ship would come up the river and they would be rich but now she knew better. She knew there would never be a ship and that Mama knew it. It was just something Mama said when she was trying to cheer them up.

"But we get by," Mama said. "Don't we always get by?"

"Sure," Abe said. "Nobody said we didn't. We were just dreaming."

"No harm in that," Mama said. "As long as we know it's a dream and don't spend all our time in just dreaming."

Becky said, "But even if you know you're dreaming, if you dream about something real special and then you know it can't ever happen, you feel bad." Talking about dreaming made her think of the book she had read at the library. She told them the story.

"That's just like a fairy tale," Cecily said. "Like dreams coming true. That's why I like fairy tales."

"Just remember, dreams don't come true unless you work for them," Mama said.

"Yeah, like shoe dreams coming true from eating potatoes and green beans," Abe said. "Yuk!"

None of them left any food on their plates.

After supper Mama and the girls began cutting out Cecily's dress. Becky and Abe did the dishes so Cecily and Maude could work on the dress. Then she and Abe worked on the picture puzzle. Nobody seemed to mind having her around. Mama didn't let her go out after supper anyway. Becky talked very little, even to Abe, so they couldn't say she was a bother.

Becky took her library card with her the next morning and then she remembered that the children's room wouldn't be open until afternoon. Why couldn't the library be open all day when school was out? She wished her friend Linda hadn't moved away. She wished she had some way to get away from all of them. Well, maybe not from Mama.

Abe came out. "Hi," he said. "I'm going to try to make some shoe money today. I'm going to that big store on Maple. I figure it's so hot some of the people over there won't want to carry their grocery bags home. I'd take you with me but it's nearly a mile away and you walk so slow, you'd hold me up."

"Who wants to go with you anyway?" Becky said. "I've got other things to do." Abe walked off as Becky was thinking, "What other things? I haven't got anything to do. I can't even go home."

Becky's First Job

Mrs. Barclay, a neighbor, came out with her three-year-old son.

"Hello, Mrs. Barclay. Hello, Freddie," Becky said.

Mrs. Barclay smiled at her and sat down on a step. Freddy ran to a car and tried to open a door.

"Don't play near the cars, Freddie," his mother said. Becky went over to the boy and led him away from the curb.

She was still trying to think of something to

do. Maybe there was some way she could make some money.

"Do you have any errands?" Becky asked Mrs. Barclay.

"Any what, dear?" Mrs. Barclay asked.

"Errands. Any jobs to do," Becky said.

"No, I don't think so, dear," Mrs. Barclay told her.

"Do you know anybody who does?" Becky asked.

"No, I don't," Mrs. Barclay said. "Well, wait a minute. Do you think you could keep an eye on Freddie? I've got so much to do inside and yet I like him to be able to play outside, too."

"Sure, I could," Becky said.

"Well, all right," Mrs. Barclay said. "I'll give you twenty-five cents an hour if you watch him for a couple of hours."

"Gee, thanks," Becky said. She would have worked for much less than that.

Mrs. Barclay stood up. "Are you sure you can do it, Becky?"

"Yes, I'll take real good care of him," Becky said.

Mrs. Barclay went up one step and turned back. "Don't let him go into the street."

"I won't," Becky said.

Mrs. Barclay went up another step. "You won't let him pick up anything and eat it?"

"I won't," Becky said.

At the door Mrs. Barclay turned once more. "Keep him in the shade as much as you can. It's such a hot day."

"All right," Becky said.

"Good-bye, Freddie," Mrs. Barclay said. "You mind Becky now, hear?"

Freddie waved good-bye to his mother. At least he isn't going to cry, Becky thought.

Now she not only had her first job but she had somebody to talk to as well. Or at least somebody to listen to her. To keep Freddie in the shade, she sat him down on the steps and told him story after story. He seemed to listen to every word. She told him about Little

Red Riding Hood, hoping it wouldn't scare him too much. Just as the wolf was about to eat Little Red Riding Hood, Freddie yawned and said, "I'm hungry."

Becky didn't know where to take him. The girls didn't want her around but Mrs. Barclay was busy, too, and she was paying. Becky took Freddie to her own apartment.

She took her key out and opened the door. "We have to make lots of noise, Freddie," she said. "Hello," she yelled. "Hi," Freddie yelled.

Becky heard the bedroom door slam. Maybe the girls were mad because she'd yelled. But how could you come in noisily and not bother anyone? It didn't make sense.

The girls came out to the living room.

"You found someone to play with," Maude said. "That's nice."

"I'm not playing with him," Becky said. "I'm taking care of him. I have a job."

"That's wonderful, Becky," Cecily said. She

added to Flo, "Becky will be taking over our baby-sitting jobs before we know it."

"You're not going to take care of him here, are you?" asked Maude.

"Of course she can take care of him here," Cecily said, "as long as they don't come in the bedroom."

"I just came to get him something to eat," Becky said. She took him out to the kitchen and gave him half a slice of bread with peanut butter on it. The girls went back to their work.

"G'bye," Freddie yelled.

"Shh," Becky told him. "Now we have to be quiet. They're busy."

She took the schoolbook from the Goodwill bag downstairs with her. She was running out of stories to tell. They walked around the block as she read to him. Becky walked in the shade as much as she could. They stopped to watch some girls playing hopscotch.

"Want to play?" one of them asked Becky.

"I'd like to," Becky said. "But I'm working right now." She and Freddie walked on.

They stopped at the fish store where some big fish were swimming in a tank in the window. Becky lifted Freddie up so he could see.

When they got back to their building, Mrs. Barclay was out looking for them. "Goodness, I didn't know where you were," she said.

Becky wished she had thought of asking her if she could take Freddie around the block but it was too late now.

"Come on upstairs and I'll give you your money," Mrs. Barclay said.

She gave Becky two quarters and a candy bar. She let Becky look at the new baby sleeping in her crib. When Becky left, Freddie cried.

Becky started upstairs to get a sandwich. She stopped and looked at the candy bar. Should she eat it now so she wouldn't have to share it? She wouldn't have much if she shared it with the others. If Maude had a candy bar,

she would eat it by herself. Becky began to open the paper. Yes, but Cecily and Flo would share candy with her even if they were mad at her. She took it upstairs.

She was so excited about the money that she forgot to make some noise as she went in. She went to the kitchen and jumped as Maude yelled, "Becky's here." Slam! went the bedroom door.

Becky put jelly on her bread and ate standing up, staring at the quarters on the table.

"What are you going to do with all that money?" Cecily said, coming in the kitchen.

"What's it to you?" Becky said.

"All right, Becky," Cecily said quietly. "I was just asking."

Becky was sorry she had spoken that way. "I'm giving it to Mama," she said.

"That's wonderful," Cecily said.

Maude said, "If Becky can baby-sit, I don't see why Mama doesn't let me."

"She will pretty soon, and this was just a

short daytime job. Becky knows she couldn't baby-sit in the evening," said Flo.

Becky looked at the candy bar on the table. "Cecily, will you cut it?" she asked.

"You eat it, Becky," Flo said. "You earned it. Isn't that right?" she asked the others.

"That's right," Cecily said. "It's too little to share with four of us."

Maude said nothing but she kept looking at the candy. Becky remembered that Maude had let her wear her raincoat. "You take a bite, Maude," she said.

Maude took a small bite. "Gee, that's good. Thanks," she said.

Becky went out with her quarters in one hand and her library card in the other. She went to the dime store and walked up and down looking at all the things she could buy with her money if she wanted to. In a way she was glad she had made up her mind not to spend the money because there were so many things she saw that she wanted. How could she begin to pick something out?

A man was taking some toy cars out of a box and putting them on a counter. "What are you looking for, little girl?" he asked.

"I'm just looking," she said. "I've got money." She showed him the quarters.

"If you tell me what it is you want to buy, I'll tell you where it is," he said.

Why doesn't he just tell me to get out instead of trying to make it sound nice, Becky thought. She looked at him angrily.

The man said, "Look, kids are always coming in here and even if they don't steal something, they tear open boxes or break things so we can't sell them. We lose a lot of money that way."

Becky left with tears in her eyes. She hadn't even touched anything. She wasn't hurting anything by just looking.

At the library she looked on all the shelves

for *The Secret River* but somebody had taken it out. She found some other books she wanted to read.

She waited on the corner for a while for Mama. "I must have missed her," she thought. She ran home. Abe went in just ahead of her.

He said to Mama, "Look, seventy cents." Proudly he handed her the money. "Maybe this will help with the shoes."

"He's been working all day," Cecily said. "He didn't even come home for lunch."

Mama said, "This money will help a lot. Thank you, Abe. But you have to eat some lunch. It isn't good for you to miss it. How many times do I have to tell you? You need it even more when you're working hard."

"Oh, that's OK," Abe said. "A lady gave me a Coke. She gave me a whole bunch of bottles to take back to the store, too. Part of the money is from that. The work wasn't hard. Most of the time I was just standing around trying to get somebody to let me carry their groceries."

"Mama, Abe wasn't the only one who worked today," Cecily said.

"Did you or Flo have a baby-sitting job, Cecily?" Mama asked.

"No, *Becky* did," Cecily and Flo shouted together, laughing.

Becky showed Mama the two quarters, but Mama didn't seem to be happy.

"Becky, it isn't time for you to be thinking about working," she said. "I want you to play, not to worry. Be a child. You'll grow up fast enough. So fast — but it was very good of you, Rebecca Jane." She tried to smile and said, "What would you like to spend it on? Striped ice cream for your birthday?"

"No, for shoes, Mama," Becky said. "Shoes come first."

Mama said, "All of my children are so good. But I wish — " She hurried to the kitchen.

Becky started to follow her but Cecily said, "Leave her alone. I'll get the towel." Mama almost never cried but when she did, there was no handkerchief big enough.

Cecily came back and the children stood together and stared at the floor. Then Flo started sniffling and the dam was burst. They all started in, even Abe, who ran to the bathroom to hide his tears.

Becky couldn't stand it. She ran into the kitchen and hurled herself at her mother and howled, "I'm sorry, Mama. Don't cry any more."

Mama held her close until Becky was quiet. Becky could feel Mama shaking and she looked up. Mama was laughing and crying so hard she could hardly speak at first.

"D-do you even know what we're crying about?" she said. She dried Becky's face and her own with the towel.

The others came in and they all started giggling and couldn't stop.

"Come on, let's start supper," Mama said.

"Beans tonight?" Abe asked.

"Spinach?" asked Becky.

"No, we'll each have a scrambled egg and fried potatoes," Mama said. "Look what I picked up on the way home. Carrots. We'll have dessert tonight, carrot sticks. And I bought some raisins to put in your oatmeal for breakfast. But I don't want you getting into them between meals. Save a few and Cecily can make bread pudding one of these nights."

That night when Becky was in bed, Mama gave her a good-night kiss and thanked her again for the money. But Becky thought she would wait a while before she tried to make more money if it made Mama act that way.

Brothers and Sisters
Are a Pain in the Neck

THE DAYS WENT BY — long, hot, end-of-summer-vacation days. The older girls still didn't want Becky around. She stayed outside as much as she could. Yet they were so nice to her when they were together that she couldn't stay mad at them for long.

Flo let her play her harmonica whenever she wanted. Abe had a job dog-walking one day and let her come along.

One cool rainy afternoon Cecily made cinnamon toast and hot chocolate for all of them and heaped cinnamon and sugar on Becky's toast. No one, not even Maude, said it wasn't fair.

Becky went back one day to where she had seen the girls playing hopscotch and made some new friends. Her sisters spent most of their time sewing. Mama sewed with them in the evenings.

While Becky was still up, Mama sewed in the living room and talked to her and Abe while the others sewed in the bedroom. When the rest of them went to bed, Mama sewed in the kitchen.

One hot night Becky was thirsty and got up, climbing carefully over Flo and Maude.

Flo sat up in bed and said, "Where are you going?"

"To get a drink of water," Becky said crossly.

"You aren't getting it in the kitchen, are you?" Maude asked.

"Mama's busy. Don't bother her," Flo said.

Maybe there was something in the kitchen she shouldn't see. Becky ran as Maude screamed, "Don't go near the kitchen, Becky!"

Abe leaped off the couch in the living room and tried to stop her. Cecily was at the door of her room and made a grab for her but Becky tore on.

In the kitchen Mama was sewing on Cecily's dress. "What do you want, Becky?" she asked.

"A drink of water," Becky said.

"I'll get it," Abe said.

They all stood watching her as she drank the water. This made them thirsty so they each had a glass.

"Well, better get back to bed," Cecily said.

Becky went grumpily back to bed. Mama hadn't said she had bothered her. But then Mama might not say it even if it was so.

She dreamed she went out to the kitchen

and opened the cupboard to get a glass. But the cupboard was full of chicken-spaghetti and striped ice cream all mixed together. It flowed out over her and covered her until she thought she was drowning. She woke up all wound up in the sheet to hear Flo saying, "Hush, Baby, it's just a dream." Flo held her until she fell asleep again.

Just before she went off, she thought she heard Flo say, "I think Mama's right, Maude. Becky thinks we're being mean. She doesn't understand and it's hard on her."

"But it's such a little while yet," Maude said. "We'll be done soon."

Friday was pay day for Mama again. Saturday Mama took Maude and Becky to the shoe store for their school shoes. Mama didn't ask what kind they wanted. They knew that school shoes had to fit and had to be strong so they would last. Becky's were brown. She liked them. She liked anything new. Her shoes were seldom hand-me-down because shoes usually wore out on whoever had them first.

"You know what I'm going to do when I'm rich?" Maude said on the way home. "I'm going to have seven pairs of shoes. I'm going to wear a different pair every day."

"I'm going to eat ice cream every day," Becky said. "Ice cream for breakfast, ice cream for lunch, and ice cream for supper."

"And get fat and lazy," Mama said.

"Well, maybe not for breakfast," Becky said. Her birthday was coming on Wednesday. She didn't dare ask her mother if there would be striped ice cream.

On Sunday she asked Cecily when they were alone.

Cecily looked away and said, "Don't ask me things like that. You know we need money for shoes."

When Becky woke up Monday morning, her first thought was — what if all this time they had been making the dress not for Cecily but for her? She told herself she would find some way to get a good look at the dress.

But when she went to the living room, there was the dress on the ironing board. It was almost done.

One look was enough. The dress was much too big for her. It was a silly idea anyway. It was Cecily who had to have new clothes.

At breakfast while Cecily cooked the cereal and Flo set the table, the girls talked about buttonholes.

"I wish Mama knew how to make them," Cecily said.

Flo said, "She said she'd ask someone at work."

"Can't we find out how and start on them and surprise her?" Maude said.

"How do we find out?" Flo asked.

Cecily said, "You could ask the lady at the dime store while I iron the dress. She should know."

"I'll go with you, Flo," Maude said.

"No, you stay here, Maude," Cecily told her.

When Flo went out, Becky went after her. She knew Flo hated to talk to people she didn't know.

Becky said, "I'll go with you, Flo. I'll ask her. Cecily shouldn't have asked you to go."

"That's why she asked me," Flo said. "She thinks if I do enough talking, I'll get so I don't mind it. Maybe she's right. But I wish you'd come along and stand not too far away in case I have trouble."

At the store Becky stood where Flo could see her in case she needed her. When Becky saw the manager going over to them, she was afraid he was going to yell at the lady for not working. Becky went over and stood next to Flo in case he yelled at her, too. But all he said was, "So that's how you make button-holes." The lady had been showing Flo how to make them on a piece of paper.

As they went out, Becky asked, "Did you mind much, Flo?"

"No," Flo said. "It wasn't bad at all because I knew you were there. Thanks, Becky."

When they reached their building, Becky stopped, hoping Flo would say she should come up.

Flo said, "Staying down? See you later, Becky."

Becky went to play with her new friends from around the block.

When she went back for lunch, the girls were in the living room making buttonholes on scraps of material. After Becky ate, Cecily said, "You want to learn how, Becky? I'll show you."

Cecily gave Becky a piece of material and started off a buttonhole. "Now why don't you go outside and make some, Becky," she said.

Just when it looked as if they weren't going

to chase her away any more, Becky thought. Would it go on like this forever?

"Don't lose the needle," Maude called after her.

Why did Maude always have to say things like that, like she was such a baby and couldn't hold on to anything? Becky was going to show them. She was going to make such good buttonholes that they'd be sorry they hadn't let her work on the dress. She went out on the steps and sewed very carefully.

She made four buttonholes, each one better than the last. Then she heard someone calling her. It was Luisa, the new friend she liked best.

"OK, I'm coming, Luisa," she said. She put the needle in the material and stuffed it up her sleeve and ran to join Luisa.

"Why didn't you come back right after lunch?" Luisa said. "I asked you to. Carmen and Lorrie went swimming and I didn't have anyone to play with. They're always going off somewhere without asking me just because they're older."

"I was going to come," Becky said. "Look, I'll show you what I've been doing." When she reached in her sleeve, the piece of material was gone.

"Oh, no, I lost it," she wailed. "Help me find it."

"Tell me what it is then, so I'll know what I'm looking for," Luisa said.

Becky told her and they soon found the material at the corner. But the needle wasn't in it. Just then she saw Abe carrying a bag of groceries.

"Abe, what will I do?" she said. "I lost a needle. Can you give me some money for another one?"

"I'm making money for shoes, not needles," Abe said.

"Please, Abe," Becky said. "I don't want the others to find out."

"How much do they cost?" Abe asked.

"I don't know," Becky said.

"I can ask my aunt," Luisa said. "We have a lot of needles."

"Can you wait, Abe?" asked Becky.

"If it's just for a minute," he said, "but hurry up."

The two girls ran upstairs to Luisa's apartment. Luisa's aunt said needles didn't cost much at all and she gave one to Becky.

Becky thanked her and she and Luisa ran downstairs. Becky showed the needle to Abe. "You won't tell the others I lost the needle, will you?" she asked him.

"Of course I won't tell," Abe said. "But I think you should tell Mama."

"I will," Becky said.

Becky took Luisa home with her. She wanted to bring the needle right away so she wouldn't lose this one. When she opened the door, she yelled, "Hello."

Cecily looked at the buttonholes and said, "These are good, Becky." Becky waited, hoping Cecily would say she could do one on the dress.

As if she knew what Becky was thinking, Cecily said, "We're going to do the buttonholes as soon as Mama comes home and says the places we marked for them are all right. Then we'll just have the buttons to do." She didn't say Becky should help with the buttonholes.

"And the hem to do over," Flo said. "It isn't right yet."

Maude said, "I'm so tired of picking thread out and doing things over. We must have sewed this dress ten times already."

"Well, it's almost done now," Cecily said.

"You'd better take good care of it," Maude said. "I want to get some wear out of it, too."

As soon as she and Becky went outside, Luisa said, "You have a lot of brothers and sisters, Becky."

"Just one brother and three sisters," Becky said.

"I wish I had some," Luisa said. "I don't have any."

"They're a pain in the neck," Becky said.

Luisa said, "I thought they were real nice."

"Sometimes they are, I guess," Becky said. "But they sure act funny sometimes."

After supper that night, Cecily put the dress on for all of them to see. Becky tried not to look at it but she couldn't help herself. It was beautiful even with the hem hanging down. She was glad of one thing. Now that the dress was almost done, they shouldn't be acting so nasty much longer.

Girls Without Bathing Caps

THE NEXT DAY they didn't ask Becky to leave. But they sat around just waiting for her to go. The day before her birthday, too. How could they be so mean? It wouldn't hurt them if she watched them just one day.

As soon as she saw Luisa, she said, "You don't know how lucky you are not to have any brothers or sisters."

Luisa asked her to stay for lunch so she didn't have to go home all day. She wasn't even going to let them know she wouldn't be home but Luisa's aunt said she should call them.

Flo answered and Becky said, "I won't be home for lunch," and hung up.

"Anything wrong?" Luisa's aunt asked. "I have one brother and when we were children we used to fight sometimes."

"It wouldn't be so bad if they'd fight," Becky said. "But they act nice and mean at the same time. They're nice when I'm there but they don't want me around."

That night Becky hardly spoke to anyone. They all tried to make her talk. Cecily showed her the dress. It was all done. So tomorrow they wouldn't mind having her around. Well, they could think again. She wouldn't stay around. And she wouldn't talk to them. On her birthday she wouldn't talk to them all day.

Cecily began to read again from the fairy-tale book but Becky went to her room. Her mother came in.

"Becky, what would you like to eat for your birthday?" she said. "I thought of having the spaghetti with chicken you like but chicken's gone up so much lately. Is there something else you like that we could have?"

Becky didn't ask for ice cream because she didn't want to make her mother feel bad having to say no. "Could we have wieners and beans?" she asked. It was a Sunday meal and she didn't know if she should ask for it. Her mother didn't seem to mind.

"Yes, that's a good idea," she said. "I tell you what. I'll give you the money and you go buy it tomorrow when it's nearly time for me to come home. Let's not tell the others. Let's surprise them. Now please come out and be part of the family, Becky. Will you do that for me?"

"All right," Becky said. She went back to the others and tried to act nice. But only for Mama.

When Becky woke up on her birthday, Flo

was standing in the room watching her. "She's awake," Flo called out.

She said to Becky, "Don't get up. Mama said this morning you should have breakfast in bed like a princess."

The others had waited for her to wake up. They all ate breakfast sitting on the bed.

If only they could always be like this, Becky thought. She remembered not to talk to them even though it was hard. But they talked so much they didn't seem to know she wasn't.

"Well, I'd better get to work," Abe said. "I'm going to help the regular delivery boy at the store up on Grove Street today. His brother's sick. A lot of people have their stuff delivered over there."

"Oh, Abe, those heavy boxes!" Cecily said.

Abe said, "It's just for a few days. Don't worry. And don't tell Mama until it's over. It won't hurt me. He has a bike and everything."

"Well, wait a minute, Abe, while we tell Becky," Cecily said.

Maude said quickly, "It was Abe's idea. He and Cecily and Flo all chipped in from money they made and Mama said they could. Becky, you and me are going swimming at the pool."

"I don't have a bathing suit," Becky said. It didn't seem real to her anyway. It was like a dream.

Maude said, "I bet my old one will fit you, and I'm using Flo's. Come on, hurry up and get dressed and let's go."

Abe had left but Becky thanked Cecily and Flo. There was no use trying not to talk now. But it wasn't fair that they never gave her a chance to stay mad at them.

"Come *on*," Maude kept saying.

The pool was fifteen blocks away but Becky would have walked five miles to go swimming.

She couldn't remember the last time she

had been swimming. It must have been before her father left. Becky tried to picture him in her mind as she often did. Sometimes she could almost picture him and other times, like now, she couldn't picture him no matter how hard she tried.

For a long time he couldn't find a job even though he looked and looked, so at last he tried to get on Welfare. They asked him if he was sick and they told him if he was able to work, they couldn't help him. So he left so the rest of them could go on Welfare.

Mama was so mad at Welfare she wouldn't have anything to do with them. It wasn't so hard for a woman to find factory work at low pay so Mama got a job even though it meant being away from them a good part of the time. Before Becky started school, a neighbor took care of her.

"How come Daddy never came back and stopped writing? Do you think he died?" Becky asked.

Maude said, "I don't know. I remember Mama talking about it to Cecily once. She said Daddy went away with big dreams. He was going to get a good job in another city and send for us to come. I guess he never did. Mama said he was ashamed he couldn't take care of us."

"Mama should have gone to the place we got the last letter from and looked for him," Becky said.

"How could she do that?" Maude said. "It costs a lot of money to take a bus somewhere. He was halfway across the country."

"Oh," Becky said. "Do you know how to swim, Maude?"

"No, but I can float. Hurry up, Becky, let's run," said Maude.

When they were inside the pool building, Becky looked around. The first thing she saw was a big sign. It said, No Running, No Beach Balls, No Water Wings, No Diving, and a long list of don'ts. It was worse than the park sign.

The last thing it said was: Girls will not be allowed in the pool without bathing caps. Becky showed this to Maude.

"That wasn't there last year," Maude said. "Anyway, they can't mean it. It's silly and it isn't fair. Why should girls have to, and not boys?"

They each paid fifteen cents for their tickets at the window and went into the women's dressing room. The room was full of rows of little closet-like places without doors. Becky and Maude soon changed into their bathing suits. They took their clothes to a lady at a counter and gave her their tickets. She put out two wire baskets for their clothes and gave them each a metal tag with a number on it. The tags were on bands and Maude put hers around her ankle. Becky did the same.

"Just a minute, girls," the lady said, when they started away. "Where are your bathing caps?"

Maude and Becky just looked at her.

"You can't go swimming without caps. It's the rule," the lady said.

Becky turned away. "I'm not going to cry," she said over and over to herself. But at the same time she was thinking how bad Abe and Cecily and Flo would feel. They had worked hard for the money, too. She bet they wouldn't be able to get the money back. Mama always said that once people got hold of your money, they didn't want to give it up.

She heard the woman say, "You can wear these this time but next time bring your own." She went to a basket where there were a few caps girls had left behind and handed them each one.

Becky thanked her and then asked, "Why do girls have to wear caps and not boys?"

"Because girls have long hair," the lady said. "Some of it comes off while they swim and clogs up the filters in the pool. Don't forget to take a shower before you go in."

As they walked over to the row of showers, Becky said, "See, it makes sense, Maude."

"No, it doesn't," Maude said. "Lots of girls have short hair. And it isn't fair. It means if you can't buy a cap, you can't go swimming. Do you think Mama would buy us bathing caps when she's trying to buy us shoes for school?"

Well, Becky thought, if this was the only time she could go swimming, she was going to enjoy it.

A sign by the showers said: Everyone must take a shower *with soap* before going in the pool.

After a few tries, they found a shower that worked. There was no soap to be seen in the soap holders.

Maude led the way out to the pool. She stepped off the edge right into the water. Becky stepped in after her. The water was freezing cold and up to her eyes. Maude pulled her to a lower spot.

110

She patted her on the back until Becky stopped choking.

"Oops, I'm sorry," Maude said. "I jumped in too deep for you."

"I'm freezing," Becky said.

"Move around," Maude told her. "It will get better in a minute. Now watch me. I'll show you how to float."

It looks easy, Becky thought. Without waiting for Maude to stand up, she tried it. Down she went and she didn't know how to get up.

Soon she felt Maude pulling her up by the arms. Becky came up choking again. Maude said, "For Pete's sake, don't try anything until I'm watching you. And keep your mouth shut in the water."

The next time, Maude held her while she floated. They were in and out of the water all morning and half the afternoon until hunger drove them home.

"I'm tired," said Becky on the way home, "but wasn't it fun?"

"I could go swimming every day," Maude said.

"That's what I'm going to do when I'm rich," Becky said.

Maude said, "I'm going to have my own swimming pool. Did you know they have them in back of some houses? I saw a picture of one once."

Becky didn't know if she should believe her or not. Sometimes Maude made things up.

"I wonder what we're going to have to eat tonight," Maude said. "Mama wouldn't tell me."

"It isn't going to be chicken-spaghetti," Becky said. I know but you don't know, she said to herself.

"Did We Do Right, Becky?"

F LO WAS IRONING when they got home. "Where's Cecily?" Maude asked.

"Mrs. Barclay had to take Freddie to the doctor," Flo said. "Cecily's taking care of the baby."

Becky hoped Freddie wasn't very sick. She asked Flo. "No, he has a cold," Flo said. "She takes him to the doctor every time he sneezes."

"Well, that's more shoe money for us," Becky said. She took the money for supper and the needle Luisa's aunt had given her and went out to play with Luisa. Mama had said she should return the needle and the others wouldn't know it was gone.

While they played, Becky held the money carefully in her hand all the time.

"If you worry so much about losing the money, why don't we buy the food now and keep it at my apartment?" Luisa asked her. They went to the supermarket and bought the beans and wieners and took them to Luisa's.

When it was time for Becky to go, Luisa handed her a small package wrapped up in pretty paper. "Happy birthday, Becky," she said.

"For me?" Becky said. "What is it?"

"Open it up and see," Luisa said.

Becky tore off the paper. It was a comb and mirror for her doll.

"Gee, thanks," Becky said. "How did you know it was my birthday?"

"You told me it was coming at least ten times," Luisa said.

"Oh, but I didn't mean — " Becky said.

"I know you didn't, silly," Luisa said. "I just wanted to give you something."

Becky thought how nice it was to have a friend like Luisa. But she didn't know what to do. Should she ask Luisa for supper? She wished she had asked Mama if she could. Maybe there would be enough food if they each ate less.

"Look, when my mother gets home, I can ask her if you can come for supper, Luisa," Becky said.

Luisa's aunt said, "Maybe some other time, Becky. When you ask your mother ahead."

"OK, I'll do that," Becky said. "Thanks a lot, Luisa."

On the way home, she saw Abe ahead of her. She ran to catch up.

"Look what I got," she said. She showed him the comb and mirror.

"Lucky you," he said. "What's in the bag?"

"I can't tell. It's a surprise," Becky said. She saw that he was carrying a smaller bag. "What have you got?"

"I can't tell," he said, just the way she had. "It's a surprise."

"For me?" Becky asked.

"No, for your great-grandmother," Abe said. "Mama told me to get it."

"Oh," Becky said. It couldn't be what she was thinking it might be and she wasn't going to think about it because then it wouldn't be. "I sure had a good time swimming. Thanks, Abe."

At home, Abe and Becky wouldn't tell the others what was in the bags. In a few minutes Mama came home. She and Becky cooked supper together. They wouldn't let any of the others in the kitchen until they were done.

When he saw the food, Abe shouted, "Man, wieners and beans. Let's eat."

"Wait a minute," Mama said.

Cecily said, "Everybody stand up."

Becky stood up too. She had forgotten about this part. They all sang "Happy Birthday" to her. She sat down quickly as they began.

"Now can we eat?" Abe said.

"All right," Mama said. "But let Becky have hers first."

When every last bean was gone, Abe said, "I'm still hungry, Mama. Isn't there anything else?"

Then Becky knew what had been in Abe's bag.

Mama took it out of the refrigerator and they all shouted at once, "STRIPED ICE CREAM!"

"That isn't what they call it at the store," Abe said.

"I don't care," Becky said. "That's what *I* call it."

"Then striped ice cream it is," Cecily said. "Let Becky have the most."

"No, all the same size," Becky said.

Flo said, "But it's your birthday."

"I know, and I want it all the same size," said Becky. "That's fair."

Becky ate the vanilla in the middle first and then the strawberry. The chocolate, which she liked best, she saved for last.

She saw that Abe saved the strawberry for last. Maude took a bite of each in turn.

When the ice cream was gone, Cecily said, "Now, Mama?"

"Now," Mama said.

Cecily got up and went to her bedroom. She came out with a shopping bag.

Another present! Becky thought. What could it be? She looked inside and saw some striped material.

"Hurry up and take it out," Abe said. "It won't bite you."

Becky pulled it out. It was a dress of pink and white and brown stripes.

She said, "It's just like — "

They all yelled again as loud as they could, "STRIPED ICE CREAM!"

"Hush," Mama said. "Remember the neighbors."

"But, Mama, you didn't buy it with the shoe money?" Becky said in alarm.

They all began talking at once.

"We made it," Cecily said. "When Mama saw the material in the store, she knew we had to get it for you."

"That's why we had to keep you out of the way," said Flo. "We made it at the same time we made Cecily's dress. First we did something on her dress and then did the same thing on this, piece by piece. We didn't have to take your dress apart as much because we learned how to do it on Cecily's dress. But your dress was harder to cut out because it's stripes. It had to be just right. Mama did all that part."

"There's just one thing," Maude said, looking worried, "and it's my fault. See, here, on the inside of this sleeve? I stuck my finger with the needle and I got blood on it. We couldn't get it out. But it doesn't show on the outside, Becky."

"I don't mind, Maude," said Becky. "Really I don't. Oh, it's so beautiful! Can I put it on? Can I?" she asked Mama.

"Yes, you can wear it for an hour," Mama said. "Then save it for school."

Becky ran to her room to put the dress on and Maude came with her.

"You should put your horse pin on," Maude said. She went to get it from the wooden box in Mama's room and came back and pinned it on Becky's dress.

"Gee, you're lucky to be the youngest, Becky," she said.

Becky started to say, No, she wasn't. She didn't like being the youngest. Then she remembered what Mama had said that night,

that they all loved her in a special way because she was the youngest. Maybe that was
so. Maude wasn't the oldest or the youngest.
Becky wanted to say something nice to make
Maude feel better but she couldn't think of
anything.

"There's some material left over," Maude
said. "I'll help you make a dress just like this
for Marjorie Lucinda. Now go *on*," she said,
giving her a push. "Show them how it looks."

Becky danced into the living room.

"Doesn't she look grand!" Mama said.

Cecily said, "It looks lovely on you, Becky."

"Don't you think it's a little long?" asked
Flo. "We could shorten it," she said quickly
to Becky.

"There's a big hem on it already," Mama
said. "This way she can wear it for a longer
time. She won't grow out of it so soon."

Becky began to laugh.

"What's so funny?" Abe said.

"I'd better wear it a long time," Becky said. "There's nobody to hand it down to."

Cecily said, "Well, I guess I could do some ironing."

"No," Mama said. "No more work tonight. You read to us from the fairy-tale book. Becky, if you're going to sit on the floor, put some paper down to keep the dress nice."

Before she began to read, Cecily said, "Becky, we wanted to tell you because we knew you felt bad — "

Flo went on, "But we thought how happy you would be to see the dress for the first time all done. They don't look like much in pieces. Then Mama said maybe it was us we were trying to make happy by keeping it a surprise and we weren't sure."

"Did we do right, Becky?" Maude asked.

They all looked at her, waiting for her to say it was all right. Becky thought of how awful it had been the past weeks when they

didn't seem to want her around. Yet, if she told them no, they would feel so bad. She couldn't do that to them. And maybe it was better this way. She was happy now, so very happy. But they were sad now, thinking they had hurt her. They must love her special, as Mama had said. And she loved them.

She looked at Mama. Mama was watching her, looking worried. Becky smiled at her.

"Yes, it was right," Becky told them.

While Cecily read, Becky sat on the floor, combing her doll's hair. She sighed with happiness. My ship has come in, she thought. My very own ship.